The Pirate Play

by Phil Kettle

Illustrated by
Melissa Webb

Get Real!
The Pirate Play

Written by Phil Kettle
Illustrations by Melissa Webb
Character design by David Dunstan

Text © 2009 Phil Kettle
Illustrations © 2009 Macmillan Education Australia Pty Ltd

All rights reserved. No part of this publication may be reproduced, stored in a retrieval system, or transmitted in any form or by any means, electronic, mechanical, photocopying, recording, or otherwise, without the prior permission of the copyright owner. While every care has been taken to trace and acknowledge copyright, the publishers tender their apologies for any accidental infringement where copyright has proved untraceable.

Published by
Macmillan Education Australia Pty Ltd
Level 1, 15–19 Claremont Street, South Yarra,
Victoria 3141
www.macmillan.com.au

Edited by Emma Short

Designed by Jenny Lindstedt,
Goanna Graphics (Vic) Pty Ltd

Printed in China
10 9 8 7 6 5 4 3 2

ISBN: (pack) 9781420278828

ISBN: 9781420278262

Contents

Introduction	5
Chapter One Boring Science	7
Chapter Two Later	11
Chapter Three Mrs Payne's Plan	18
Chapter Four Are You Ready?	22
Chapter Five Show Time!	24
Chapter Six Act One	26
Chapter Seven Act Two	38
Chapter Eight Act Three	48
Chapter Nine Act Four	56
Chapter Ten A Little Bit More	61
Let's Write	64
Jesse and Harry Present	66
Word-up!	68
A Laugh a Minute!	70

Introduction

The one on the right looking amused is Jesse Harrison. The one on the left, also looking amused, is Harry Harvard. The one sitting in between Jesse and Harry with his head resting on his desk and his eyes closed is their prehistoric friend, Rocky Rockman.

The one standing up is Mr Zimmer. Mr Zimmer is the science teacher at Average Primary School. And the one at the back, dressed as a pirate, is Samantha Smithers. So why is Sam dressed as a pirate? Well, if you keep reading this book, pretty soon you'll find out.

Chapter One

Boring Science

> **A REMINDER FROM THE AUTHOR**
>
> As you know, Harry and Jesse's amazing adventures usually begin with them speeding home on their skateboards after spending another day playing practical jokes and getting into strife and trouble at Average Primary School. BUT THIS ISN'T A NORMAL ADVENTURE.

Jesse, Harry and the rest of Mrs Payne's Grade Five students were sitting in Mr Zimmer's science class.

Mr Zimmer's science class was the same today as it was every other day – BORING! When the Grade Five students asked Mr Zimmer why science was so boring, he simply shrugged. "Science isn't boring and anyone who says it is will be staying behind this afternoon in detention," he frowned.

The Grade Five students answered as one. "We all LOVE science. We think it is the best subject taught at Average Primary School. And you, Mr Zimmer, are the BEST science teacher in the entire world."

"I know," Mr Zimmer replied, and then he went on to explain how the solar system works. Ten minutes later, the entire Grade Five class fell asleep.

Suddenly the students were woken by the squeaking, scratching, squealing sound of the school PA system.

The Grade Five students snapped to attention as Principal Dorking's voice boomed out, "This is your leader, Principal Dorking!"

The class responded as one.

"Please listen closely to this very important school message."

boring

"As you know, it is that time of the year again…"

"...time to start rehearsals for the annual Average Primary School stage show!" boring

"And I have some very good news for all those students who think that they might like to be thespians this year," continued Principal Dorking.

> **AUTHOR NOTE**
> THESPIAN means ACTOR!

"I'm going to be the producer!" Principal Dorking finished. "Me, Principal Dorking, not only the greatest school principal of all time, but possibly the greatest actor of all time too – that never got a break. Auditions will be held at lunchtime in the assembly hall. I suggest that you line up as soon as the bell goes for lunch."

Chapter Two

Later

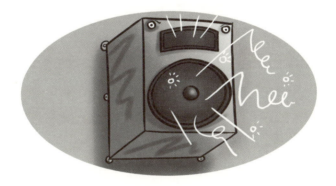

When the lunch break finished, Mrs Payne returned to her classroom. Suddenly the squeaking, scratching and squealing of the PA system woke up most of the students who were still asleep.

"CAN YOU HEAR ME? This is Principal Dorking speaking! I'm assuming that the PA wasn't working before lunch. Only one student turned up for auditions for the annual Average Primary School stage show. Thank you, Samantha Smithers."

boring

"But there's no need for the rest of you to worry. There will be another opportunity to audition after school today. As an added incentive, students that are chosen to be in my play will be given two days off from school when the play finishes."

hooray!

"I always thought that I could be a great actor," Jesse said to Harry.

"And I always thought that I could be a great *Shakespearean* actor," Harry replied seriously.

"You thought you'd be a great *what*?" Jesse asked.

"A great *Shakespearean* actor," Harry repeated, rolling his eyes. "You know, performing in one of Shakespeare's famous plays, like *Hamlet*."

"Well, I don't know who Shakespeare is. But I do know that if Principal Dorking chooses us to be actors in his play, we're going to get two days off school!" Jesse declared.

"And that would be REALLY great!" laughed Harry.

Suddenly Mrs Payne, who had overheard Jesse's conversation with Harry, had a brilliant idea.

> **AUTHOR NOTE**
> Mrs Payne did not have brilliant ideas very often!

"Class, I need you to listen to me very carefully," she said. "I think that each and every one of you would be an amazing actor in Principal Dorking's play. So, my wonderful, delightful and incredibly talented students, we've got to come up with an amazing plan to ensure that you are all chosen to perform in Principal Dorking's play!"

"Maybe we could lock Principal Dorking in the classroom with Lenny 'the Stink' Edwards, and only let him out if he promises to put us all in his play," Jesse suggested.

"Hmmm, I think maybe we need a different plan," Mrs Payne answered dreamily. "But I like your ideas."

"Students, I think I've got it!" Mrs Payne announced a few moments later.

"Is it devious?" asked Harry.

"And dastardly?" asked Jesse.

"I think it might be," smiled Mrs Payne. Then she carefully explained her plan to ensure that every student in Grade Five would be cast in the annual Average Primary School stage show…

Chapter Three

Mrs Payne's Plan

Immediately the Grade Five class started to work on Mrs Payne's plan. All the students were excited.

One hour later, the results of all their hard work were visible for the entire class to see and admire.

"Well class, all we have to do now is give the birthday card to Principal Dorking," said Mrs Payne, with a satisfied look on her face. The students hoisted the card aloft and she led them out of the classroom and along the corridor to Principal Dorking's office.

Samantha Smithers was getting some books out of her locker.

"Where are you going?" she asked Harry and Jesse.

"Principal Dorking's office," said Harry, blushing.

"And we're not even in trouble!" said Jesse, smiling.

Mrs Payne knocked on the door. As soon as Principal Dorking opened it, Mrs Payne led the class in a rousing version of 'Happy Birthday to You'. It was followed by three cheers for Principal Dorking and an equally rousing version of 'For He's the Best Principal in the Entire World'.

"Thank you Mrs Payne and students, but it's not my birthday," said a stunned Principal Dorking.

"But Principal Dorking," Mrs Payne explained. "We think that you deserve to have a birthday *every* day of the year."

"And we just want to show you how much we appreciate you," said the Grade Five students together.

Principal Dorking looked serious and puffed out his chest.

"Grade Five, you are by far the *best* class of students in all of Average Primary School. I think you should ALL be in my cast for this year's amazing annual Average Primary School stage production!"

Chapter four

Are You Ready?

> **A NOTE FROM THE AUTHOR**
> If this story had an extra two hundred and two pages, I could tell you all about the rehearsals, but there isn't enough room. So, what I will tell you is this. Jesse, Harry and Rocky all got lead roles in the play. Samantha Smithers was the leading lady. By opening night, a massive crowd had packed the Average Primary School hall in anticipation of an incredible stage show.

Chapter five

Show Time!

The Pirates of Average!
A Play by Principal Dorking

Cast

Susan — Samantha Smithers

Captain Dodgy — Jesse Harrison

Scrubby — Harry Harvard

Crabby — Rocky Rockman

Mogga — Lenny 'the Stink' Edwards

Sea Monster — Principal Dorking

Mother Monster — Mrs Payne

The Pirate Crew — The Rest of Grade Five

Chapter Six

Act One

Susan ☠ Yo, I'm Susan, the smartest pirate sailing the seven seas. 'Susan' isn't a proper pirate's name. One day I'll find myself a really good pirate's name! I've just arrived at this beach hideaway. Some of the world's most fearsome pirates spend their holidays here.

Susan ☠ What's wrong with being smart? Anyway, today is my BIG day. I'm finally going to spend a day with the world's most fearsome pirates. I've dreamed about this day since I was little.

Captain Dodgy ☠ Shut up and line up, me hearties! And hurry up about it, or else I'll make you all walk the plank! Right, we need a crew for a treasure hunt on Scumbury Island. We need to find some money to buy new swords. I'll take Scrubby (because his mother always packs a good lunch) and Crabby (because he has a really cool parrot).

Susan ☠ I'm so excited! This is the first time I've tried out to be part of a crew on a pirate ship and Captain Dodgy has the best pirate ship on the seven seas. I hope he picks me too!

Captain Dodgy That's it then. The rest of you, get lost!

Susan Wait! What about me?

Scrubby No way, smarty-pants. You're a girl!

Captain Dodgy You had better stay here and let the real pirates go. We don't need girls on our ships, especially when there are sea monsters around. We don't want you to get hurt. You'd scream – like a girl.

Susan Maybe I'll never be a proper pirate. Boo, hoo!

Mogga What's this boo-hooing I hear? You need to toughen up, kid!

Susan ☠ No one wants me to be a pirate because I'm a girl…and I'm smart. Everyone laughed at me and said I'd be scared. But I'm not scared of anything, even sea monsters. And I wouldn't cry… boo, hoo! Oh, who am I kidding? I'm a girl. BOO, HOO, BOO, HOO, BOO, HOO!

Mogga ☠ Are you finished? Do you feel better now?

Susan ☠ Actually, yes. I always feel better after I jump up and down and cry, thank you.

Mogga ☠ One day you'll realise that being smart is not so bad, and neither is being a girl.

Susan ☠ Well, I refuse to move from this spot until that day. And if anybody tries to move me, I'll kick them in the knee cap.

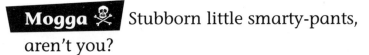 Stubborn little smarty-pants, aren't you?

Scrubby SHOCK, HORROR!

Susan What's happened, Harry? Whoops, I mean Scrubby.

Scrubby The ship is gone – totally destroyed. Never to be seen again!

Susan Totally destroyed! How?

Crabby A gigantic sea monster!

Susan You've got to be joking. The big brave pirates couldn't stop a sea monster?

Crabby ☠ We tried but the monster was too big and powerful. The ship is gone forever!

Susan ☠ So, how come you survived?

Crabby ☠ I tried to save the ship, but I swam to shore when the ship went down.

Scrubby ☠ I hid under my bed when I saw the monster coming. Then I hitched a ride back on a dolphin.

Captain Dodgy ☠ Who would believe it? Our ship is gone, and the sea monster took the rest of the crew!

Susan ☠ Wow! So what are you going to do now?

Captain Dodgy ☠ Maybe we'll go and have a milkshake. Is there anything else we can do?

Scrubby ☠ Maybe I'll go and open a drink stand in Average Park. I could sell drinks to the tourists that come to watch Concorde in his nest.

Susan ☠ You do that and you might end up at the bottom of the pond wearing a pair of lead boots. But being the heroes that you are, you can't just give up. You must save the rest of the crew!

A REMINDER FROM THE AUTHOR

You might recall that in another book in this series, **Snooping Snoopalot**, Samantha Smithers opened a lemonade stand in Average Park. She sold drinks to the tourists who came to watch Concorde (Rocky's pet bird) in his nest – at the top of the tallest tree in Average Park. Samantha made LOTS of money, so she doesn't want anyone else's drink stand competing with hers!

Captain Dodgy ☠ Well there's no way I'm going out to sea again. Not with that gigantic sea monster out there. Actually, it looked a lot like Principal Dorking – sorry, I didn't mean to say that!

Susan ☠ You're not pirates – you're just a couple of really big CHICKENS.

Captain Dodgy ☠ If you think you're so smart and brave, why don't you deal with that sea monster yourself, SMARTY-PANTS!

Scrubby ☠ Best of luck to you!

Susan ☠ Someone has to save the rest of the crew! Follow me, Crabby. We're going to save some pirates.

Chapter Seven

Act Two

Sea Monster Isn't life great? It's been a busy day. This morning I sank another pirate ship and captured another pirate crew. It's pirate legs for tea tonight! But what's that I see? A small rowboat is approaching the beach...

Crabby ☠ What makes you so sure we can rescue the other pirates, Susan?

Susan ☠ Because I'm Stubborn Susan! I'm smart and I'm a girl and girls can do anything they put their mind to.

Crabby ☠ Yeah, and what are you going to put your mind to now?

Susan ☠ Rescuing the other pirates, of course!

Crabby ☠ And how are we going to do it?

Susan ☠ Hmmm, I might need a bit more time to think about that!

Crabby ☠ What's that roaring noise?

Susan ☠ What roaring noise?

Crabby ☠ *That* roaring noise!

Susan ☠ I hear it, but I don't see it.

Crabby ☠ Ahhh! Run!

Susan ☠ Crabby, get back here! Oh well. I can do this alone. SHOW YOURSELF, SEA MONSTER! I'm ready for you.

Susan ☠ Captain Dodgy, what are you doing here?

Captain Dodgy ☠ I was feeling bad, leaving you and Crabby all alone to fight the sea monster.

Sea Monster 🌊 Hey, there's Captain Dodgy! Run little pirate, before I make you do detention! Sorry, I mean before I put you on my barbeque and turn you into pirate steak!

Captain Dodgy ☠ No, you better run before I tell everyone that you tried to sell Concorde's egg! Sorry, I mean before I tell everyone you tried to eat the rest of our pirate crew!

Sea Monster 🌊 What? You can't do that! And if you do, you'll have detention for the rest of your life. Sorry, I mean I'll feed you to my pet shark!

AUTHOR NOTE

You might recall that in that other book I mentioned before, **Snooping Snoopalot**, Principal Dorking wanted to steal and sell Concorde's egg!

He didn't succeed, of course.

Susan ☠ You can throw Captain Dodgy into detention – sorry, I mean you can throw him to your pet shark – but I'm not afraid of you!

Sea Monster 🐚 Why aren't you scared?

Susan ☠ Because I'm a girl and I'm smart and I can do anything.

Sea Monster Hmmm, smarter than the average pirate I see!

Susan You bet! Now, why did you destroy Captain Dodgy's pirate ship?

Sea Monster Oh, that wasn't me. That was my mother.

Susan Then I need to have a good talk to your mother!

Sea Monster You can't do that.

Susan Why not?

Sea Monster Because she won't talk to you. She'll just capture you and tie you up with the others, so we can eat you for dinner later.

Susan That's terrible!

Sea Monster Don't worry, those pirates are just getting what they deserve.

Susan I won't hear of it. Take me to your mother – or else!

Sea Monster Or else what?

Susan I'll...I'll...

Sea Monster You'll...you'll...what?

Susan I won't tell you my really cool secret.

Sea Monster Secret? What secret?

Susan I knew it. Principals just can't resist a good secret. Sorry, I mean sea monsters!

Chapter eight

Act Three

Sea Monster Right then. I'll take you to my mother. This way please!

Captain Dodgy Hey Scrubby, what are you doing here?

Scrubby I came back to join the fight!

Susan Stop! What are you doing?

Scrubby I've killed the sea monster, I'm a hero!

Sea Monster Who did that? It hurts!

Scrubby It was her. She did it! And I'm off!

Susan Here, let me help you.

Sea Monster Why would you want to do that?

Susan Well, I kind of like you.

Sea Monster You do? Nobody likes me much, because I'm a Principal. Sorry! I mean a sea monster. Why do you like me?

Susan Because you're big and strong — and you write the school reports!

Susan ☠ Here, let me help with that. On the count of three, I'll pull out the sword. Are you ready?

Sea Monster 🐚 Maybe.

Sea Monster 🐚 Hey, here's my mother now!

Susan ☠ One, two...

Sea Monster 🐚 ...where's three?

OOOUUUCCCHH!

I guess that was three!

Susan ☠ I got it out! That wasn't too bad, was it?

Sea Monster 🐟 Susan, meet my mother. Mother, this is Susan.

Mother Monster 🐟 How lovely! Another pirate for our collection.

Susan ☠ Actually, that's what I need to talk to you about. I need you to release all those pirates you captured from Captain Dodgy's ship.

Mother Monster 🐟 But why? They've made a rubbish dump of the sea.

Susan ☠ So, you're mad at them because they litter?

Sea Monster 🐟 Yes! Pirates make a lot of rubbish!

Susan ☠ But you can't go around smashing up pirate ships. That's littering too!

Mother Monster 🐙 Good point – I think. You're no dummy!

Susan ☠ That's right. I'm smart! And if I promise that those pirates will never litter again, will you let them go?

Mother Monster 🌀 Maybe. But can I trust you? You're a pirate too, after all.

Sea Monster 🌀 She's not like other pirates, Mother. She helped me when I was hurt.

Mother Monster 🌀 Okay then. We'll let the pirates go!

Chapter Nine

Act Four

Captain Dodgy ☠ Wow! That was awesome. Well done Susan!

Susan ☠ All the pirates are free!

Scrubby ☠ Wow! You saved them! How did you do it?

Susan ☠ I promised the sea monster and his mother that all you pirates would stop littering the sea.

Scrubby ☠ Hmmm...that's a fairly big promise!

Captain Dodgy ☠ That was a brilliant move, Susan. I never thought a girl could be so smart or so brave. And you did it all on your own too.

Susan ☠ Smart girls can do anything they put their mind to, Captain Dodgy.

Captain Dodgy ☠ I see that now, Susan. How would you like to be first mate aboard my new pirate ship?

Scrubby ☠ But Captain Dodgy, I'm first mate!

Susan ☠ First mate? Save it for Scrubby. I'd rather be captain of my very own pirate ship!

Captain Dodgy ☠ Three cheers for SUSAN!

Scrubby ☠ Hip-hip-hooray! Hip-hip-hooray! Hip-hip-hooray!

Susan ☠ That's *Captain* Susan to the lot of you! And now get out of here you scurvy dogs, or I'll make you all walk the plank!

Chapter Ten

A Little Bit More

The final curtain closed on the annual Average Primary School stage show. The massive crowd that had packed the Average Primary School hall rose to their feet as one…

clap clap clap clap whoohoo!! clap whoohoo clap whoohoo!! clap clap

"Hey Harry, that was pretty good," said Jesse. "As soon as we get back to our tree house, I reckon we should use our time machine to visit that Shakespeare guy. He might be able to give you a few more acting tips."

"Great idea, Jesse. But I think it's you that needs the tips!"

Let's Write

Finding an Idea

Writing a play is a little different to writing a story. For a start, you have to remember that the audience will be *watching* the play, not reading it. So remember to 'show it, don't say it'. For example, if a character is confused, write a stage direction that has them scratching their head.

Most of your play will be made up of dialogue – the words the characters say to each other. The dialogue must do two things:

- give the audience enough details to move the plot along
- tell the audience about the character who is speaking.

You might like to give your characters a feature that the audience will be able to see or hear – like a funny walk or a crazy laugh.

Planning a scene

A play is made up of many scenes. Scenes are kind of like the chapters in a book – something happens in each scene that moves the story along and leads to the next scene. A good way to write a play is to break it down into scenes. You can write the key idea for each scene on a card. Then go back and write the dialogue and stage directions for each scene.

So open up your creative-writing book and start working on a play. You could team up with a classmate to do this. Good luck!

Jesse and Harry Present

About the Author

Jesse: Phil, I reckon that you must have been in a play when you were at school.

Phil: Not only was I in a play, but I was the absolute star!

Jesse: So you had the lead role?

Phil: No, I mean I was the star in the play.

Jesse: How could you be the star in the play if you weren't the leading character?

Phil: Well, when I said I was the star, that's exactly what I meant. The play that I was in was called 'Twinkle Twinkle Little Star' and I played the star.

Jesse: You're really funny!

Phil: I know!

About the Illustrator

Harry: Ahoy there Melissa, how would you like to be a pirate and sail the seven seas with us?

Melissa: Not much....get sea sick....bllluerk.

Harry: Is it hard to draw pirates and all their gear?

Melissa: Not too bad, lots of dashing jackets, hats, parrots, belts, buckles and stripy things.

Harry: Well, you did a great job!

Word-up!

Assembly: confusion multiplied by the number of students present in the school hall

Compromise: the art of dividing a cake in such a way that everybody believes he or she got the biggest piece

Detention: the future tense of trouble

Dictionary: the only book where the finish comes before the start

Lecture: the art of transferring information from the notes of the teacher to the notes of the student

Smile: a curve that can set a lot of things straight

A Laugh a Minute!

What's the best thing to take to the desert?
A thirst aid kit!

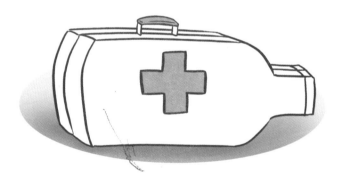

Why did the lazy girl want a job in a bakery?
So she could loaf around!

Where do snowmen go to dance?
A snowball!

What happened when the wheel was invented?
It caused a revolution!

Did you hear about a mad scientist who put dynamite in his fridge?
He blew his cool!

Who was the first underwater spy?
James Pond!

Other Titles in the Series

The Time Machine

Ferret Attack

The Trouble with...

Just Another Day

Planet Snoz

Big City Museum

The Flying Machines

Snooping Snoopalot

The Last Day